KU-444-598

This Bing book belongs to:

. . . .

Copyright © 2019 Acamar Films Ltd

First published in Great Britain in 2014 by HarperCollins *Children's Books*,
a division of HarperCollins *Publishers* Ltd, 1 London Bridge Street, London, SE1 9GF

3 5 7 9 10 8 6 4 2

ISBN: 978-0-00-797947-9

Based on the script by Lead Writers Ted Dewan and Lucy Murphy and Team Writers Mikael Shields and Philip Bergkvist.

Adapted from the original books by Ted Dewan and using images created by Acamar Films, Brown Bag Films and Tandem Ltd.

Edited by Neil Dunnicliffe.

Designed by Anna Lubecka.

No part of this publication may be reproduced, stored in a retrieval system or transmitted
in any form or by any means, electronic, mechanical, photocopying, recording or otherwise,
without the prior permission of HarperCollins *Publishers* Ltd

www.harpercollins.co.uk

All rights reserved

Printed in China

Ducks

HarperCollins *Children's Books*

Round the corner, not far away,
Bing is feeding the ducks today.

It's a **sunny day** and Bing,
Flop and Sula are at the **park**.

They've brought bags full of
food for the **ducks**.

"Look," says Bing.
"A duckie!"

"That's not a duckie," says Sula, "that's a **pigeon**."

Bing asks Flop why the pigeon doesn't fly away.

"Because the statue is very, very good at staying **still**," says Flop.

"Oh, statue still," says Bing.

As they run to the pond, Bing and Sula shake their bags and sing.

"Duck-duck-duckie! Wak-wak-wak!"

Scared by the noise,
the ducks on the pond
all flap away.

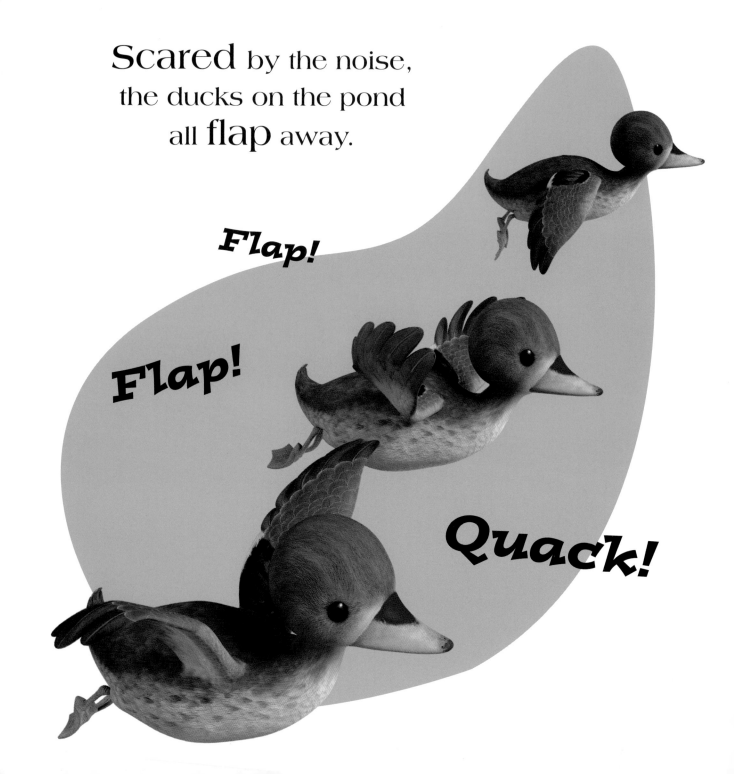

Flap!

Flap!

Quack!

Bing is disappointed.
"Oh, why have the ducks gone?"

"I know, Bing!" says Sula.
"Let's give them some food."

Bing throws a **big** handful of food onto the pond. He waits.

"Look, Bing!" whispers Sula. "There's one. "

"Where?!"
shouts Bing.

The duck **bobs**
down under
the water.

Flop points at the statue
and whispers,

"Remember Bing,
statue still and
shhh. Then the
ducks will come."

"OK!" Bing whispers back. He stands statue still.

Up pops the duck again from under the water.

"A duckie!"
yells Bing.

Whoops!

The duck flaps
off again.

"Why won't that duckie come to me?" asks Bing.

"Because you're all noisy, Bing. He gets scared when you go

blulalulah!"

says Sula.

Bing watches Sula. She is quiet and still
and feeding lots of ducks.

"Aw, Sula's got
all the duckies!"
says Bing.

Bing **throws** some food on to the pond.

A little duck swims over from Sula's
side and **gobbles** it up. Ooh!

Splash!

The ducks scatter.

"I got a BIG duck!"
says Bing.

Sula takes a step back. "Bi-ing, that's not a duck.
That's a goose! And he's eating all the food!"

The goose **flaps** his
wings and **jumps**
out of the water.
He is coming
for more food.

Bing and Sula
run away
and hide.

Flop takes Bing's empty bag. He blows into it,

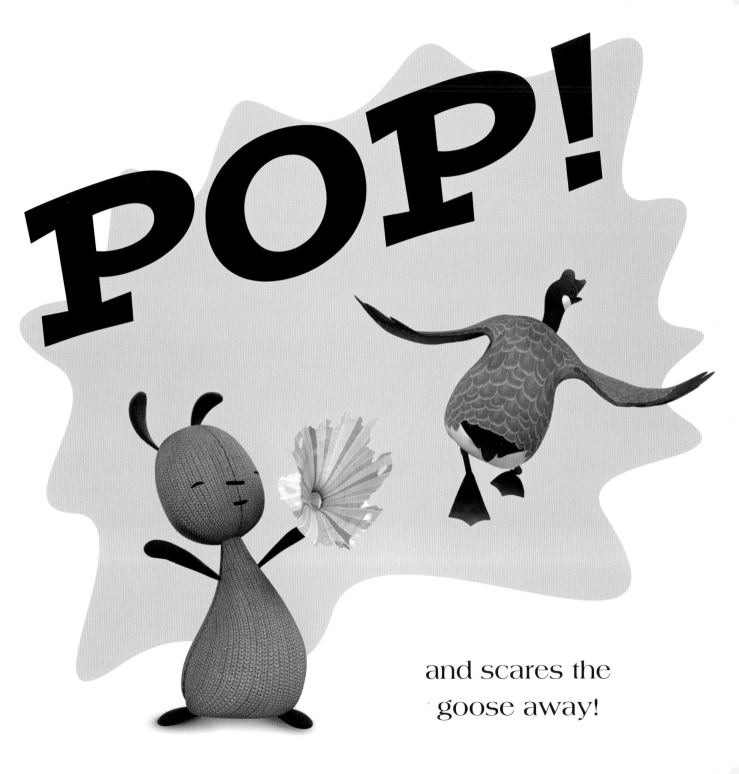

POP!

and scares the
goose away!

"Ohh, all of the ducks have gone," says Bing.

"All of the ducks?" asks Flop.

A small duck hops on to the path.

Bing and Sula stay **very** still. **Statue still.**
And **very** quiet. Bing holds out some more food.
The duck comes closer. It nibbles at the food!
"It tickles!" giggles Bing.

Nibble!

Nibble!

Nibble!

"Good for you, Bing Bunny."

Hi!

We went to feed the **ducks.** But Sula had **all** the ducks...

...so Flop said 'stay statue still'. Then the ducks would come to me too.

But a **big goosey** came and it went

waaarggghhh

and that was scary.

So Flop went **pop** and goosey flew away.

If you're very quiet and statue still, then the duckies will come.

Feeding the ducks...

it's a Bing thing.